flying memos

Published by MQ Publications Limited
12 The Ivories, 6–8 Northampton Street, London N1 2HY
Tel: 020 7359 2244 / Fax: 020 7359 1616
email: mail@mqpublications.com

ISBN: 1-84072-605-9

1 3 5 7 9 0 8 6 4 2

Printed and bound in Italy

flying memos

and other office antics

BY LISA SWERLING & RALPH LAZAR

MQP

RON ALMOST SUCCEEDED IN HIDING THE FACT
THAT HE WAS COMPLETELY COMPUTER ILLITERATE.

Executive toy
of the week:
Automated
paper-rocket
generator.

AUDIT

COMPANY
ACCOUNTS

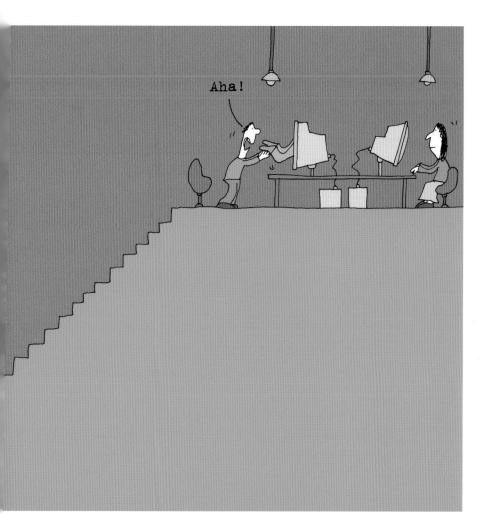

AND SUDDENLY THE KEYBOARD GRINNED.

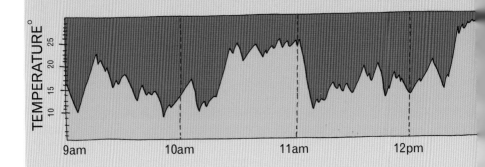

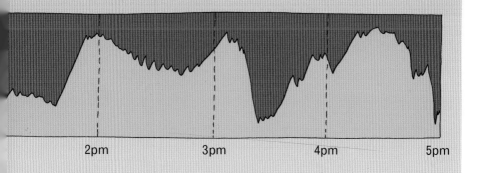

Finance terms explained:
"Irrational exuberance"
Derek reacts to the
market rally.

I think Edna
has been drinking
too much coffee.

ROD CALLED UP SOMEONE FROM THE TECH
SUPPORT GROUP AS HIS PC SUDDENLY
SEEMED TO BE IGNORING HIM.

I think you
may need a
restructuring
consultant.

ADVANCES IN GENETICS: HUMANS DESIGNED TO DEAL WITH VOICEMAIL.

HUMAN
RESOURCES
DEPT:
QUEUE HERE
FOR JOB
INTERVIEWS

SYDNEY TOKYO BONN LONDON N.Y.

Finance terms explained:
'Commodity derivatives'
(Case study: the coffee market).

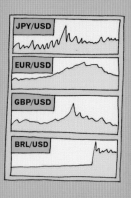

I think you might want
to reassess your strategy
of sending staff on evening
accountancy classes.

...beep beep...
...beep beep...

ACME COMPUTER OUTLET

This software comes with all the latest tools!

Great, I'll take it!

Thesaurus!

1

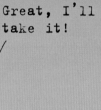

2

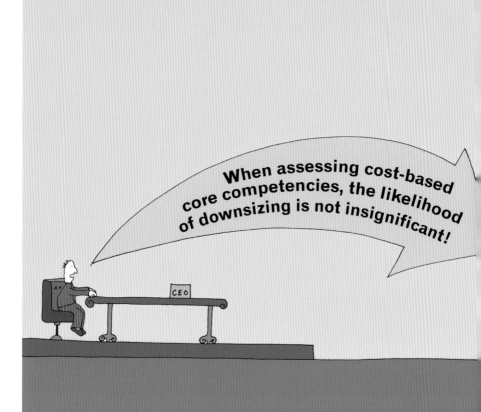

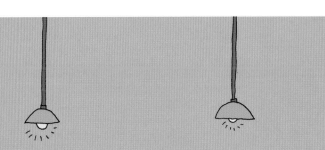

Hmm, head massage.

Such a nice boss.

Lovely day, isn't it?

Finance terms explained:
"Out-of-the-money options"

(1) Rob bank.
(2) Borrow from father-in-law.
(3) Go traveling.

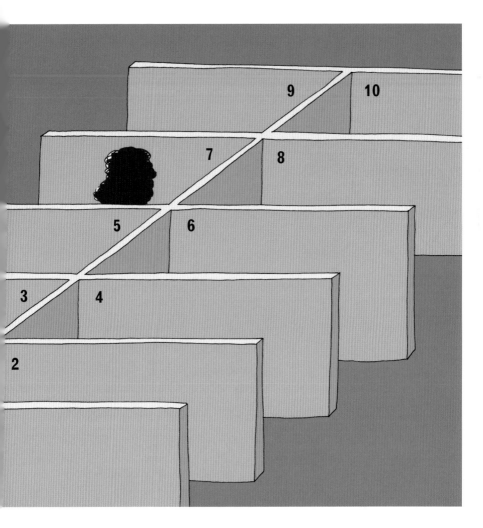

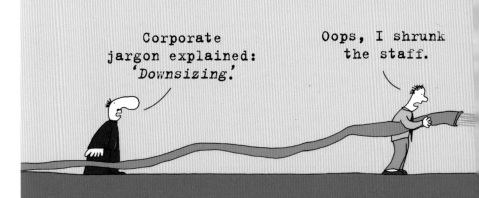

ABOUT THE AUTHORS

Ralph Lazar and Lisa Swerling are currently
based in the UK. Other titles created by them
include Harold's Planet and Hotdog-Dog.